THIS BOOK BELONGS TO

BETTY HAYS

THREE SAXON NOBLES
AND OTHER VERSES

THREE SAXON NOBLES
AND OTHER VERSES

By Jack Prelutsky
Pictures by Eva Johanna Rubin

THE MACMILLAN COMPANY
COLLIER-MACMILLAN LTD., LONDON
COLLIER-MACMILLAN CANADA LTD., TORONTO, ONTARIO

There was a tower, long ago
That reached up through the air
And in it lived three lovely girls
With beautiful brown hair.

They'd open up their windows wide
When day had just begun
And calling through the morning mist
They'd wake the sleeping sun.

There once was a bean
A little white bean
Who journeyed to England
To visit the queen.

England was closed
And the queen was in Rome
So the little white bean
Turned around and sailed home.

"Good morning mister snail"
Said the keeper of the jail
"I hope that all is well
With you and with your shell."

"Oh yes," the snail replied
"And would you like a ride?"
"Oh no," the keeper said
"I think I'll walk instead."

Three Saxon nobles, a count and two earls
Galloped to France just to see the young girls
They'd hardly arrived, when the fortunate three
Spied eleven young maids growing high in a tree.

Their cheeks were all rosy, they all wore fine clothes
With colorful buttons and beautiful bows
"How strange to see girls grow in such an amount"
Said the three Saxon nobles, two earls and a count.

Cock-a-doodle-doo
The train is coming through
It was to come at one o'clock
And now it's after two.

The driver lost his map.
The wind blew off his cap.
And since he was already late
He stopped to take a nap.

Four furry kittens with
  great green eyes,
Lived in a house
  of very large size,
Lived with their friend
  the little gray mouse,
Who cooked and cleaned
  in the very large house.

She swept the floor
  and went to the store,
Dusted, darned and
  answered the door,
Washed and ironed for
  the four furry kittens
Polished their shoes and
  knitted them mittens.

When winter snows fell round their house
The four furry kittens would treat the mouse.
They'd pull her around the fields all day,
Cozy and warm in her own little sleigh.

We have a splendid carriage,
Our horse is swift and brown,
And every Sunday afternoon
We ride about the town.

We have a handsome coachman
Who drives us through the park.
He buys us cake
    and chocolate milk
And gets us home by dark.

Robinson, Robinson
Didn't you smile
When your balloon
Took you up for a mile?

Robinson, Robinson
Didn't you frown
When you discovered
You couldn't come down?

Jumping Jane and Jumping John
Jumping with their slippers on
Jumping fast and jumping slow
Jumping high and jumping low
Jumping bottom jumping top
Jumping start and jumping stop
Jumping sun and jumping rain
Jumping John and Jumping Jane

Helen loves her heavy hat
With its feathers fluffed and fat.
Even when she goes to bed
Helen keeps it on her head.

Aunt Anna had a wondrous plant,
Its trunk was straight and slim
And flowers of the rarest kinds
Grew out of every limb.

Aunt Anna also had a tree
With leaves of every hue,
Bright leaves of gold,
    dark leaves of green,
And leaves of red and blue.

Atop this tree there was an egg
And when it hatched one day
A fuzzy rabbit popped right up
And quickly flew away.

E * D
N *

E.J.Rubin 1967

Library of Congress catalog card number: 69-14272

Printed in the Federal Republic of Germany
First American edition published 1969

First Printing